D0777176

Project Wheels

Jacqueline Turner Banks

Houghton Mifflin Company
Boston 1993

Library of Congress Cataloging-in-Publication Data

Banks, Jacqueline Turner.
    Project wheels / Jacqueline Turner Banks.
        p.   cm.
    Summary: While helping to raise money to buy her classmate Wayne a
motorized wheelchair, eleven-year-old Angela finds her relationships
changing with her four best friends.
    ISBN 0-395-64378-3
    [1. Moneymaking projects — Fiction.   2. Wheelchairs — Fiction.
3. Physically handicapped — Fiction.   4. Friendship — Fiction.
5. Schools — Fiction.   6. Afro-Americans — Fiction.]   I. Title.
PZ7.B22593Pr   1993   92-10843
[Fic] — dc20   CIP
                          AC

Printed in the United States of America

VB   10   9   8   7   6   5   4   3   2   1

To my parents who paid for the library book I lost when I was four. To my friends and relatives who, for many years, have listened to all the plots. To Regina, Geoffrey, and Jeremy for their patience and inspiration. And especially to Reginald for his support and love.

· *Chapter 1* ·

Friends

"Guess what?" Judge said to me as we were walking to our class. He was smiling his "this is a joke" smile, so I was afraid to answer. Since his brother, Jury, answered, I didn't have to worry.

"We have a sub."

"I think he was talking to me," I told Jury. It's always like that with the two of them. No matter who else they're talking to, basically they're talking to each other. Judge and Jury Jenkins are twins. I've known them since kindergarten. They're the brothers I've never had — but I'd never tell them that.

"She's great, she doesn't mind if you talk or pass notes."

"Yeah, as long as you don't disturb the rest of the class."

They both were grinning, like any minute they

were going to tell me the punch line. I figured I'd play along.

"That's good to hear," I said. "Nothing like an easy sub to make a Friday perfect."

We started talking about something else, and I forgot about their telltale grinning. Also, the substitute teacher had let them take a break after first period, and that's always a good sign. Half of my class starts school just after eight and leaves at two o'clock. The other half starts around nine and leaves at three. I have late math, which means I'm supposed to start at nine, but my GATE (Gifted and Talented Education) class is at eight. In other words, I have an extra class each day. I know it's confusing, but you get used to it. They had to start this early and late stuff when the school became overcrowded.

When we entered the classroom the twins didn't waste any time getting to their seats. Also, I noticed that most of the others in the early math group hadn't taken a break. That was when, I thought, I had figured out why the twins were grinning; they had pulled a fast one on the sub. She didn't give them a break. After first period a series of bells ring just as they do before it. These bells are for the late math kids, but they're also for kids going and returning from speech class, GATE, and band. There's a lot of activity in the classroom with kids coming and going, and it's usually confusing for a substitute. Especially when you add the kids who get up and leave just because they know they can get away with it. It's an old trick. They've been pulling it off since fourth grade.

I looked at the substitute teacher. She was watching the minute hand on the clock as if she had money on whether or not the tardy bell would ring on time. She sure didn't look like the easygoing type. Her dress was basic teacher: a long flowered skirt, tucked-in solid-colored blouse, and the required cardigan sweater on her shoulders. She reminded me of that teacher in the Miss Nelson books — Viola Swamp. She even wore half-glasses on the bridge of her nose.

"I have a great idea for the Christmas project," Faye Benneck whispered to me just before the bell rang. Faye sits next to me. In fact, since my name is Angela Collins, Faye has sat next to me in every class for the last six years. A lot of times the teachers change kids around after they get to know us, but our regular teacher, Miss Hoffer, says that we're sixth-graders now and we should be able to behave ourselves no matter where we sit.

Part of me didn't care about Faye's "great idea" — let her tell it, that's the only kind of ideas she has. Another part was just a little curious. I wondered why she didn't tell me in GATE class. Our GATE teacher calls talking "creative expression."

"What is it?" I whispered back.

Faye shook her head as if to say not now. The boys had already set me up to believe that in spite of her expression, the sub was cool. I figured nobody had told Faye about this strange-looking woman's liberal policies.

"It's okay, tell me," I whispered a little louder.

"Young lady, who told you that you could whisper in my class?"

I looked right up into two nostrils being pinched by granny glasses. Her bright flowered skirt seemed to be flapping in a sudden wind. I got so confused, I really believed she was asking me a legitimate question.

"Judge and Jury," I answered. The whole class cracked up. Miss Wonderful Substitute thought I was getting fresh with her.

"Get out!" she yelled.

I was shocked. For the first time in my life a teacher was yelling at me, Angela Davis Ibadan Collins, and she was kicking me out of class. I was afraid to move. I didn't think my legs could support my weight. Tears were building up behind my eyes, but I'd be hanged if I'd let her see them.

4

"Now, young lady!"

I got up. The legs were wobbly, but they were working. Fixing my eyes on the door, I started the longest trip by foot I'd ever taken. Just before I reached for the doorknob, from the corner of my eye I saw Jury Jenkins trembling with laughter.

I stood in the hallway for a few minutes before it occurred to me that maybe I was supposed to go somewhere. Since it was my first experience with banishment, I didn't know. I tried to remember if Judge or Jury ever mentioned what you're supposed to do when you're kicked out of class. They've had considerable experience in that area.

I knew I wasn't supposed to go home because I couldn't remember anybody ever being out for the rest of the day. Also, my key was in my purse and my purse was still in my backpack in the room. I peeked into the classroom. The substitute was going on with social studies as if nothing had happened.

I'd heard kids say they had to go see Mr. Carlisle, the vice principal. I decided to go see him. Even if I was wrong, Mr. C. would know what to do. Vice was his business.

I like Mr. C. This isn't something I like to say too loud. Nearly everybody I know hates the poor man. They call him names related to his short height or his cowlicked blond hair. But Mr. C. made a friend for life in me when I was in the third grade.

My teacher had recommended me to take the GATE test. I went to Mr. C.'s office, and for two hours I answered questions on the oral exam. When the test was over he seemed happy. I was happy too. Two hours is too long for any test, oral or written.

"Angela, you're the kind of student who makes the crap worthwhile," he said.

I had absolutely no idea what he was talking about, but I couldn't wait to get back to class. I wanted to tell the twins that Mr. C. had said "crap." After that, Mr. C. began to greet me by name whenever he saw me.

So I went to see my buddy, Vice Principal Carlisle. At first the secretary, Mrs. Keats, didn't want to let me see him because I didn't have a hall pass. I don't know about other schools, but hall passes are a big deal at my school. Some of the kids say Mrs. Keats hates the black students. They say she was working at Faber Elementary when it was all white. Apparently, even after all these years, our presence is still a problem for her.

"It's okay, Mrs. Keats, it's always a pleasure to visit with Angela."

My man, Mr. C., tell her about it! I can't explain why it happened, but as soon as I sat down in his chair, I started crying. I told him everything between loud, ugly sobs.

"Okay, dear, come with me," he said as he handed me a tissue.

We went back to the classroom. Mr. C. asked the substitute to step out into the hall. I couldn't hear what they were saying, but at one point they started laughing in that way adults do when they find a kid's humiliation humorous.

The sub led me back into the classroom. She smiled at me a couple of times during the day, but I iged — ignored — her.

I rolled my eyes so hard at Judge and Jury I got a headache. They knew exactly what they were doing. I don't know why I still trust those two. They've been doing things like this for years.

At recess Faye apologized as if it were her fault. I didn't blame her, but her apology was typical Faye behavior. She always does the right thing, even when her heart isn't in it. Sometimes it can be very annoying.

I like Faye, I really do, but sometimes she can be a real pain. She's so competitive. Some people say I am too. I'm not competitive, but I do have a "healthy appreciation for the pursuit of excellence." My father describes me that way. He's a teacher over at the teacher's college. He's good with words.

I didn't think about Faye's idea for the Christmas project again until I was walking home from school. I realized that she hadn't told me what it was. I decided if it was important, she'd call me, and if not, she'd tell me in school on Monday.

I was just about to turn onto my street when I heard the boys running up behind me. I know them so well, I can recognize the sounds of their feet crunching through October leaves. I refused to turn around.

"We know you heard us calling you." That was Judge talking.

It's easy to hurt Judge's feelings, and since seeing Judge hurt is the only thing that affects Jury, it's like killing two birds with one stone. They fell into step beside me.

"Come on, Angela, give it up. If it happened to anybody else you would've laughed," Jury said.

"Don't say nothing to me, Jury Jenkins. I saw you laughing when that . . . that woman kicked me out."

"It was funny. Wasn't it funny, Judge?"

"It was funny. Angela, you should have seen your legs shaking. . . ."

"Yeah, and when she peeked back into the

room, like a little lost puppy . . ." The boys
stopped walking and started laughing.

As I got farther and farther away from them,
I could hear them rehashing every embarrassing
detail. By the time I was standing on my porch,
trying to find my key in my junky purse, I was
laughing so hard I was afraid I wouldn't get to
the bathroom in time.

When I stepped out of the bathroom, the telephone was ringing.

"Angela, this is Judge. We never got a chance
to tell you about Faye Benneck's plan."

"Put Jury on the phone."

As soon as I heard Jury say hello, I slammed
the receiver down.

· Chapter 2 ·

T.G.I. Monday

When I heard my mother's first wake-up call, I actually said, "Thank God, it's Monday." When you're feuding with your best friends, what's the sense in having a weekend?

On Friday night my parents rented a video, but there was so much talking in it, I fell asleep. Saturday I played with the little third-grader down the street, but if anybody ever asks, I was baby-sitting. Saturday afternoon my mother asked me to go to the mall with her and that was kinda fun. When we got back, I went with my father to the campus. While he worked in his office, I sat in the quad and looked at college kids. Looking at college kids used to be one of my favorite pastimes, but they were all in groups. Groups reminded me of friends, and friends reminded me of Judge and Jury. Sunday morning we went to church, and the rest of the day was one of those lazy Sundays that my parents love and I hate.

My women's-size-six feet hit the cold hardwood floor when I heard the threatening tone in my mother's second wake-up call. I dragged myself to the window. I'm not one of those people who have to look outside when I wake up, but I thought I could smell snow in the air. I was surprised to see the glow of the morning sun bouncing off the remnants of my mother's flower garden. It never occurred to me that it was October and it never snows in Kentucky in October. The only reason I was interested in the weather is because I was tired of my summer clothes.

"Hurry up, girl. If you're late, don't expect me to write a note," my mother said in her usual harried voice. She was standing in my doorway.

"Okay, Momma."

But she didn't leave the spot where she stood. I noticed an odd expression on her face that my eleven-year-old mind couldn't interpret.

"What's wrong, Momma?"

She crinkled her nose the way she does when she's trying to do some serious thinking.

"Does it smell like rain to you?"

"No, I smell snow in the air."

She looked excited, pleased to have a daughter

11

whose nose could make such a wrong interpretation.

"Well, okay, I'll go along with that. At least I'm not the only crazy one. The man on the radio said to expect dry weather, temperatures in the eighties."

"I guess that means I can't wear my new corduroy skirt?"

My question snapped her back to reality. She rolled her eyes at me for asking such a dumb question, checked her watch, and nearly ran out of the room.

It's always like that with me and my mother. One minute we'll be talking like best friends, the next minute she'll seem to realize that she's talking to a kid and the thought will annoy her. Her flip-flops don't bother me, because sometimes she can be a weird best friend. But she's always a good mother.

When I say weird, I don't mean in the scary sense or the dangerous sense. She's just too thoughtful sometimes. She'll ask me stuff like, "If suddenly you were a bird, where would you fly first?" If I'm in a mood to talk, we can go on and on for hours talking about places we'd like to see from bird's-eye level.

On the days I don't feel like talking, all I have to say is something like, "I'd fly over to the vet's to see if I could get some help." Those answers will end, in a blink of an eye, our strangest conversations.

My mother is always running late. "It's twenty minutes to eight," I said to the closed bathroom door. My mother is the director of a community center. She's supposed to be at work at eight.

"Go find my navy blue shoes."

Her bed was made and the room was spotless. As far as I'm concerned, that's her problem — she wastes too much time in the morning doing unnecessary things. Her shoes were lined up neatly at the bottom of her closet. I slipped on her right shoe. It was a little loose, but at the rate I'm growing, I figure I'll outgrow her shoes by spring. It's not fair.

In Plank, Kentucky, where we live, petite, busty women with well-shaped calves and tiny waists are considered cute by the general population. Forget about fashion magazine models. Cheerleaders, homecoming queens, and first-choice prom dates in Plank are built like my mother. I'm built like my father.

I'm five-foot-five already, and I won't be twelve until December twenty-seventh. My mother says mine is the body of the future and hers is the body of the past. I don't know exactly what she means, but it seems to me that bodies shouldn't go out of style. Who decides these things anyway? If my body goes out of style in the next generation, will I be allowed a trade-in?

At least I have good skin and hair. Some of the kids are starting to get teenage zits already. My skin is a little oily, but so far it's clear. I'm darker than both of my parents. I never thought about my skin tone much until this year. We'd been studying genes and heredity. I asked my mother how I came to be darker, and she went off.

"Your skin is beautiful. It's a perfect coffee. Why, what is this about?" she asked. I could see she was getting her "concerned Mom" wrinkle in the middle of her forehead. I guess she thought somebody had been teasing me about my skin color. Parents must think that school is just one big teasing festival.

"It's nothing," I told her. "We've been studying genes at school."

"Oh. I've always thought you had my sister's color, Aunt Cea."

I thought about it. She was right. I did have my aunt's skin color. That was all the information I needed, but I could tell my mother had something else she wanted to say.

"I read somewhere that there are thirty-two distinct shades of African-American skin. I believe there's more, but if that number is true, I'll bet we have half of those shades in my family."

I just nodded. Talking about skin color wasn't my idea of a good time.

I have a lot of hair. It's not long like Faye Benneck's. Faye is always flipping her hair off her neck. It drives me crazy. Talking to Faye is like talking to one of those bobbing-head dolls. She says a word, she flips her hair. Word-flip-word-flip, over and over again.

My hair is full, thick, and almost shoulder length. It would take a hurricane to blow it off my neck, and that's just fine with me.

"I'm putting your shoes by the door."

"Thanks, baby."

She didn't make me late for school. At seven-fifty I was locking the front door. Faber Elementary is three blocks from my house. I enjoy the morning walk. So much so that I feel sorry for the kids who get rides to school. There is no school busing in my town. Kids go to school in their own neighborhoods. I know it's not like this in Louisville and Lexington, but in our little town we do things the logical way. It wasn't always like that. My mother tells a funny story about when she moved here from Decatur, Georgia. She was just starting high school, and the boundaries had just recently been changed for racial equality in the schools. The story is not meant to be funny, and it bothers my father when I laugh.

"You just don't understand, Angela. There's no way I would've moved to Kentucky if the movement hadn't happened," he says.

My father is from Milwaukee. I don't quite understand how he does it or why it works, but he jabs my mother sometimes just by saying, "I wouldn't know about that, I'm from Milwaukee!"

My mother gets really mad when he says it. It must be one of those games adults play. I've visited both Milwaukee and Decatur lots of times. I can't imagine what it is my father thinks he has over my mother.

I noticed the twins just as I turned onto the school's street. I almost called out to them before I remembered I wasn't speaking to them.

I saw Judge's pace slow down. I imagined him telling Jury to apologize, and I imagined Jury saying that it wasn't his problem if I couldn't take a joke. Judge stopped walking. I didn't speed up, but I didn't slow down either when I saw that he was waiting. Jury continued to walk ahead, his steps slow and stubborn.

"Angela, are you still mad?" Judge asked.

I kept walking. What a dumb question. Had anything changed since I slammed the phone down in Jury's ear?

"We didn't expect you to get in that much

trouble. We figured you would talk and the sub would tell you to stop — that's all."

"Just tell her no harm, no foul," Jury shouted back at us.

Lately Jury's been using a lot of clichés. I wouldn't be surprised if he didn't have a book of them somewhere in his house. Usually his silly expressions make me laugh. Jury makes me laugh, but I wasn't ready to give in, even with Judge watching me with his big sad eyes. He's so sensitive, in a non-Jury-type way, that I worry about him sometimes.

"Give it up, girl. You're crying over spilled milk," Jury shouted back.

"Tell your brother if he's got something to say to me, he can come back here and tell me himself."

Judge smiled and repeated my message. Jury stopped walking and waited for us to catch up with him.

"It's always darkest before the dawn," he said, as a greeting.

I started laughing. "That's the stupidest one yet, what does it have to do with anything?" I asked.

"They don't have to make sense. He just likes to say them. It's really starting to get on my nerves," Judge volunteered.

"Did Judge tell you we were sorry?"

"Yeah."

"Good. You want to play pom-pom tackle?"

"No, you know I hate that game."

"Well, we have a blood match waiting. Let's go, Judge."

They ran ahead of me. With only seven minutes left before the first bell, I didn't know how much of a blood match they could hope to play. Pom-pom tackle is a stupid game all the fifth- and sixth-grade boys at my school play. It doesn't seem to have any rules except everybody tackles the person with the pom-pom. A pom can be anything — a hat, a glove, anything small enough to carry that can be seen by everybody.

I know I gave in too easily, but Jury wasn't going to say he was sorry. And there's no challenge in making Judge suffer.

I saw the twins again just before the bell rang. A whole group of boys was walking toward the sixth-grade classes, closely followed by Mr. C. Pom-pom tackle is a forbidden game, and they were probably in trouble. I suspect three out of four boys in school who break arms, fingers, or legs break them playing that stupid game.

Mr. C. stopped and talked to the group for a moment, then he let them go to class.

"Angela, I forgot to tell you something," Judge called out to me as I started for GATE class.

"You better hurry."

· Chapter 3 ·

Faye's Idea

The bell rang for early math. We knew we only had five minutes to get to our classes.

"Jury, you tell her. You talk faster."

"Okay, you know how Miss Hoffer said we were supposed to be thinking about our Christmas project?"

I nodded and so did Judge, as if he was hearing it for the first time.

"Well, this year instead of doing some stuff for a bunch of kids we don't even know, Faye said we should buy Wayne DeVoe a motorized wheelchair."

I stopped walking and looked at the grinning brothers. That was a good idea. It was such a good idea I was sorry it wasn't mine.

"Sounds okay," I said. There was no need for me to show too much enthusiasm; it wasn't their idea either. "We'll talk about it later." I ran ahead to catch up with Tommy M., another kid in my GATE class. "If you two don't hurry, you're going to get lunch detention," I shouted back.

I thought about Faye's idea through the first half of GATE. She's in the class too, but we didn't get a chance to talk about it. How does she keep coming up with these great ideas? You should have seen her fifth-grade science fair project.

A motorized wheelchair for Wayne — wow.

Wayne DeVoe started going to Faber in the fourth grade. The first time I saw him sitting in his little wheelchair back at the time-out table, I wanted to cry. He wasn't being punished or anything, but the time-out table was the only one in the room that didn't have a chair attached to it.

He was as small as a first-grader. His red T-shirt hadn't been a bright red in several years, and he was wearing jeans that somebody else must have worn out at the knees. His hair was a dirty blond and his eyes were a muddy combination of gray and brown. He was the first kid in a wheelchair I had ever met.

I know everybody likes to pretend that disabled people are the nicest people in the world, once you get to know them, but that's not true. I learned in the fourth grade that people in wheelchairs are just like people walking around on two feet. Some are nice and some aren't. Wayne DeVoe was in the latter category.

Our fourth-grade teacher went through great pains to prepare us for Wayne. She explained that he was paralyzed from the waist down as a result of an early childhood injury. She added that there was absolutely nothing wrong with his sight, hearing, or any of his other senses. We had a lot of questions, and she took the time to answer them. When she finished, we were eager to meet Wayne — to welcome him with open arms.

Wayne hadn't been in the school three hours before he stuck Tommi Block with a pencil lead. Everybody thought that getting stuck with a pencil lead was the leading cause of death in elementary-school-age children. Poor little Tommi was hysterical right up until the moment her mother arrived to carry her home. We still tease her about it.

Wayne wasn't even punished. Our teacher was going out of her way to be nice. We knew she was mad; her bottom lip was trembling.

"Sometimes it's difficult to be the new kid," she explained to the class, with that bottom lip going a mile a minute.

"If he comes near me with a pencil, I'm going to break his arms," Jury said at recess.

"Yeah, and we'll break his arms if he comes

near you, too," Judge assured me. This was before my first major growth spurt and during their gallant period.

I wasn't sure if I wanted to see the little fellow with broken arms *and* paralyzed legs. Tommi Block was a crybaby. Nobody told her to go back to the time-out table and start messing with Wayne. Maybe she had lead poisoning coming.

I left the twins playing pom-pom tackle and looked for Wayne. I found him on the west field watching a basketball game.

"Wayne?"

"Yeah?"

"I'm Angela Collins."

"So what?"

"So you better make a friend fast because they're turning on you." I waved my hand at the kids in front of us to indicate exactly who was doing the turning.

"Let them turn. This is my sixth school in four years; friends are the last thing I'm looking for."

"Six schools! I didn't know there were six elementary schools in Plank."

"Did you know there's a world outside of Plank?"

"Sure."

"Well, there are schools in that world, brainiac!"

"What makes you think I'm a brainiac?" I asked, choosing to ignore what may have been sarcasm.

"I'm paralyzed, not stupid!"

"I know, I'm sorry. The teacher said you were able-bodied in every other way." As soon as I said it I knew it was a dumb thing to say. I just wanted to use the word "able-bodied."

"I knew it!"

"You knew what?"

"I knew the teacher had prepared the class for me."

"So?"

"So how would you like it if a teacher knew you were coming and took it upon herself to prepare the class for dealing with a nig — black girl?"

I was sitting on the ground next to his chair. I looked up at him. The little fellow was right. But if he ever made the mistake of calling me a nigger, he had better hope the twins got to him first.

"She meant well," I said in defense of my teacher.

"My daddy says the road to hell is paved with good intentions."

I stood up. That was one of the most clever things I had ever heard a kid say. Unless Tommi

Block was to die from lead poisoning, Wayne DeVoe was probably all right.

"Come with me," I said, grabbing the handles of his wheelchair.

"Where are we going?"

"I want you to tell my friends Judge and Jury what you just said about good intentions."

"Judge and Jury?"

"Don't ask."

We went over to the field where the boys play pom-pom tackle. None of the boys who gathered around seemed to understand what Wayne's quotation meant, but they were awfully impressed with his use of the word "hell." Before too long, they were pushing him around the yard. Somebody hid the pom-pom — in this case a piece of lining from a jacket — in his lap.

As far as I know, Wayne's family has moved within the city twice since fourth grade. The first move took him out of our boundaries, but one of the teachers drove him to school every day. None of us were supposed to know that. The next move put him back in his old neighborhood.

Wayne is the next to oldest of seven children. There's talk that his parents fight and his dad drinks. Seven kids in one small house is reason enough to have a bad attitude, but if any of the other stuff is true, I figure Wayne has a right to be a jerk sometimes.

GATE class was a lot of fun. One of the kids brought in a book of Plexers. They're pictures that make a popular phrase. For example, the word "school" at the top of a box would mean high school. That's an easy one. The class was able to figure out about half of them.

After class Faye waited for me by the door.

"Did the twins tell you about my plan?"

"Yeah."

"Well, what do you think?"

"It sounds okay. How much do those motor-ized chairs cost?"

"I don't know."

"Where are we going to get the money?"

"I don't know. That's why I wanted to talk to you. You're a good organizer. We figured you'd tell us what to do."

"We?"

"Jury, I mean the twins — both of them — we were talking about it. Judge says you're the best when it comes to making a plan."

I beamed. She was hustling me and she was up to something, but I loved the flattery.

"All right, let me work on a plan."

· Chapter 4 ·

The Organizer

I've been thinking, maybe when I grow up I'll be a person who organizes other people. There must be a job description that starts out: Wanted, ORGANIZER, must be able to get knee deep in other people's business . . .

After school on Monday, Judge, Jury, Faye, and I met with Miss Hoffer, our teacher.

A teacher can have too much colorful, educational, inspired junk hanging in a classroom. When I'm sitting at my desk, I can bury my head in my work and ignore the attack. But standing at her desk, I couldn't help but wonder if Miss Hoffer's walls weren't a cry for help.

She had posters of books, inventors, "Americans Who Made a Difference," a tribute to the world's religions, and a scattering of Sesame Street and Disney characters offering advice on various subjects. If that wasn't enough, she had six mobiles hanging from the ceiling.

"What a wonderful idea! I'm so blessed to have such caring students."

I noticed the twins backing away from her desk. Miss Hoffer has been known to have hugging attacks.

She's a good teacher. A few years ago she became a born-again Christian. There's a lot of born-again Christians in my town. Most of the time, you can't tell from their actions. They have to tell you or you have to read it on their bumper stickers. Miss Hoffer isn't like that. She lives the life she claims to believe.

She doesn't have any children of her own, and, surprisingly enough, she's from one of the most racist families in town. Her brother owns the ShopAll store. He treats his black customers like potential shoplifters and follows them all over the store. Her father, the late Big John Hoffer, was a legendary racist. And yet they don't come any fairer than Miss Hoffer. If there's anything wrong with her, it's her tendency to get too involved in her students' lives.

When Miss Hoffer is happy, she hugs. The guys always act like they hate it, but I suspect some of them really like it. You can't have too many hugs in your life.

"But how will we manage? They must cost hundreds. We've been allotted fifteen dollars for expenditures per classroom," Miss Hoffer explained. I could see doubt creeping into the fine lines on her forehead.

"Let us work it out," Faye begged with big girl-next-door eyes. Sometimes she's just too cute.

"If we can't pull it off, we'll still have plenty of time for a food can drive."

"Or a trip to Children's Hospital."

"But we want to keep this to ourselves. We're afraid if we tell Wayne or the rest of the class, they'll be disappointed if we can't raise the money."

"We can tell them we're raising the money for another cause. Too many cooks will spoil the stew."

"I can see that you boys are really committed to the project," Miss Hoffer said after Judge and Jury's rapid-fire comments. "What do you think, Angela?"

"I'd really like to see Wayne with that chair, Miss Hoffer. We have two months and I think we can do it. With the four of us and Tommy M., we can get all the details nailed down. Our class has always been the best at fund-raisers."

Miss Hoffer rested her head in her hand. I don't know why it required this much thought, but maybe she knew something I didn't know.

"How can I help?" she finally asked.

Faye told Miss Hoffer that I was going to figure out what had to be done and delegate duties
to the others. I could see she liked using the word
"delegate." We decided we would tell the class
that the money was being raised to make a nicer
Christmas for a child our own age.

"Is that going to be enough information? Don't
underestimate your classmates."

"Believe me, Miss Hoffer, Faye is probably the
only kid in class who has thought about it even,"
Judge said.

"Yeah, who thinks about Christmas when we
haven't had Halloween yet," Jury said.

I looked at Jury as he spoke. Last summer my
Decatur cousin, Rose, spent two weeks with me.
She went on and on about how cute the twins
were. The first week she fell in love with Judge,
the second week was Jury's turn. It was a very
weird time for me. Sometimes I see it, but most
of the time they don't look particularly special.
Sure, they have great haircuts, decent clothes,
and their skin is still clear, but I know them too
well.

I know that Judge is still a little afraid of the
dark. Sometimes Jury will bite his nails until they
bleed. Both of them have an unnatural fear of
birds, planes, or anything flying over their heads.
Nobody at school knows this, but it's the reason

they don't play football. When the old pigskin sails toward them, they freeze. Maybe it looks like a big bird or something. I know Jury is a little sharper in the brains department, but he'll wear a pair of socks until they stand on their own. Judge is the kindest person I know, but if you cross him he's ruthless. I'm probably the only girl in the sixth grade who loves them both without ever being in love with either of them.

I suspected that Jury was Faye's real purpose behind this Christmas project. Lately I'd been getting vibes that told me Faye had a crush on Jury. He's the cuter of the two. He's about half an inch taller and he has a smile that gets him out of a lot of trouble. Faye has always been the type to come up with a plan, but she's not the type to share the glory. It's another way that we're alike. First she dumped the grunt work in my lap, and she told the twins before she told anybody else. Things just didn't fit. Judge and Jury are not the kind of guys you would ask to work on a school project. They're the kind of friends you'd call to hang out at the mall with you.

With Miss Hoffer's blessing, it was full speed ahead. The four of us started walking home. Faye chatted endlessly about how happy this surprise was going to make Wayne and how we were going to have regular meetings to discuss details. The boys got involved in an impromptu game of kick the can, and for the most part they ignored us.

Faye turned off two blocks from school because she lives in the "subdivide." That's what everybody calls it, but it's called Rolling Greens Lane on the map. It's the newest part of Plank.

I live in College Park and so do the boys, but they live close to the downtown border. This might sound like a big hike, but we're all within ten blocks of each other.

Just as Faye started walking away, she turned on her heels and called back to us.

"Jury, I don't remember if I said good-bye — did I?"

"Yeah, you said good-bye to all of us."

"Well okay, 'bye again," she sang out. She actually sang the words.

I wasn't going to tease Jury, but I made the mistake of looking at Judge. We both cracked up.

"'Bye again," Judge sang out in imitation.

"Don't start in on me, man."

"That's right. He can't help it if he's just so darn cute," I teased as I pinched his cheek.

"What happens to you girls in the sixth grade?"

"What do you mean?" I asked.

"That's the same girl who almost got me kicked out of school in June. Remember when she went to Mr. C., just because I used her sweater as a pom-pom?"

"We did rip her sweater," Judge said.

"Whose side are you on?"

"Don't go getting all mad at me, I didn't tell her to start liking you!"

"I should tell Angela who calls you nearly every night."

"If you do, I'll tell her about the note."

I doubt if they noticed when I turned off at my street. What did I care about telephone calls, or notes, or arguing brothers? What concerned me was my two best friends were keeping secrets from me. The question is what happens to boys in the sixth grade? What happens to your best friends in the sixth grade?

· Chapter 5 ·

Family

My father's car was in front of the house. It wasn't three-thirty yet and he was home. My father teaches at the Southwestern Kentucky Teacher's College. His last class is over at four, and he's usually in his office until six. As I took the steps two at a time, the thought occurred to me that something could be wrong.

The front door was unlocked, but that's not so unusual in Plank. I never knew how much people value locks until I spent a couple of weeks in Milwaukee with my father's parents. They were forever asking each other, "Did you check the locks?"

We do have crime. Sometimes the college kids get a little crazy or somebody's car is stolen. My parents' friend Rex is a policeman. He said that whenever there's a property crime in Plank they round up the usual suspects. I thought that was a great line until my mother told me it was from an old movie.

My father was sitting in the living room, which was odd enough. We never use that room unless we have company. Most of our family time is spent in the kitchen/breakfast nook area. I live in what visitors always call a "great old house." It's okay, it's certainly big enough for the three of us, but I'd rather have a "cute new house." Faye lives in a new house and I love it. There's not an inch of wasted space in her house, there're no oak cabinets to polish every time relatives are coming, and it's probably not cold all winter and hot all summer.

"What are you doing here?" I asked my father.

"I live here."

"*Dad*-dy!"

"*An*-gela!"

He loves to tease me. He even does it when I have friends over. "Daddy, you know what I mean."

"Yes, I do. You mean you're not happy to see your dear old dad."

I sighed loudly. He smiled.

"All right, my impatient one. We're having a campus-wide blood drive for the kids who were hurt in that car accident last weekend. Angela, have I talked to you about drinking and driving?"

"Yes, every time somebody gets in an accident."

"It bears repeating periodically. Anyway, I gave blood earlier in the week. I didn't need to be on campus, so I decided I would come home and get you to go running with me."

"You've started back running?"

"Last week, I told you," he said as he started up the stairs. He didn't say where he was going, but since he was still wearing his teacher clothes, I assumed he was going to change. He didn't wait for me to answer; I guess he assumed I wanted to go.

I did want to go, but I felt I should turn him down. It was a pride thing. A few weeks back I heard the tail end of a conversation between my parents. I don't know what they said before the part I heard, but it must have been about me. Just before I walked into the kitchen, I heard my father say, "Okay, Marilyn, I'll try to start spending more time with Angela."

"It's the only way to approach this, Marcus. You two were always so close."

I walked into the room and the conversation immediately switched to family gossip. I felt like crying. Why would my mother have to ask my father to spend more time with me? He used to like me.

I thought about it for days. It's not that I hadn't noticed that my father was avoiding me, but I figured it was a stage he was going through. Sometimes I prefer one parent over the other, so it stands to reason that parents would have the same kinds of stages. The thought that he really didn't like me anymore never crossed my mind.

"Is that what you're running in?" my father asked me when he returned. He was wearing the blue-and-green sweats I bought him for Christmas. I believe I have the best-looking parents of any kid I know.

"I'm going to change shoes."

"Well, move it!"

I ran upstairs and changed from my regular no-name sky-blue canvas shoes to a pair of name-brand running shoes. The cool kids who were sixth-graders when I was a fifth-grader started the no-name club. They refused to wear anything with somebody else's name on it. If the best-fitting jeans had a label on the back, they would take it off. Sometimes they'd replace it with a label of their own name. They let a few fifth-graders join, but it was very selective. They never asked me. When they went on to the middle school, four kids in my grade continued the tradition. One of them asked me to join this year. It's very informal, no dues, no meetings, no name brands. I was asked to join the day after my mother bought me a pair of fifty-five-dollar running shoes.

"Finally," Daddy said when I returned. "I was beginning to think you were getting to be as slow as your mother."

We walked to the college track. Several times I've suggested to my father that we should run to the track, run around once instead of twice, and then run back. Each time he says it's a good idea, but then we end up doing the same old thing.

"I haven't seen Judge and Jury around much lately. Where are they?"

"At home, I guess."

"Don't tell me you're not friends anymore, not after all this time."

"I still like them."

"But?"

"But they've been treating me different . . ."

"Differently."

"Differently. They keep secrets from me. I don't understand it," I said. "I haven't done anything to them." It was the kind of thing I would normally say to my mother. I guess the after-school incident got to me more than I thought.

37

"I think I have an idea about it."

"What?"

"Have you looked in the mirror lately?" he asked. I nodded.

"You're changing, I mean your body is changing. Maybe the boys can't see you in the same old light anymore."

At first his words embarrassed me. I walked a few feet in silence. The more I thought about it, the more I felt I had to say something.

"Daddy, that's just plain stupid. I'm the same person."

He laughed. "Yes, it is stupid, but I think I'm right. I understand what the boys are going through. I went through the same thing."

"When you were a kid, you mean," I said.

"No, when *you* were a kid. An eleven-and-a-half-year-old, to be exact."

"What do you mean?"

"I know you've noticed that we don't do as much stuff together as we used to."

"Yeah, I figured you were going through a stage."

He started laughing and stopped right there in front of the science building to hug me.

"I was going through a stage. I was going through your puberty and it was making me crazy. Your mother noticed that I wasn't hugging you as much as I used to. She thought we'd had an argument. It's very hard to see your little buddy grow into a young woman. It's probably not easy for the twins either."

"Daddy, do you ever wish you had had a boy instead of me?"

"I can't deny that I've thought about having a son, but I never wanted to replace you with a son. Your parents are still young, it could still happen."

"Ugh, Daddy, ple-ease!"

· Chapter 6 ·

Faye's Halloween Party

Faye wanted to refer to it as "Project Wheels," so now every time I wanted to say something to her about the surprise I had to use that code name. I didn't know what was happening to that girl. She used to be so normal.

In less than a week, I gave everybody on Project Wheels their assignments. The twins were supposed to get information on a candy sale and Faye was going to work on the dummy project, the one we'd pretend to be doing, so the class wouldn't spill the beans to Wayne. Tommy M. and I were going to get estimates on motorized wheelchairs so we could compare the prices.

Tommy came over to my house after school on Wednesday. We decided to call the wheelchair places together. The day the boys told me about

40

Faye's plan they told me she wanted to include Tommy in on it. He's been with the four of us since kindergarten; he would have been my choice too. Tommy Masaki is one of the smartest, nicest people I know, but that's not why everybody likes him. He's so funny, he makes everything fun. Whenever the teacher wants us to work in groups or teams on a project, everybody wants Tommy M. on their team. Miss Hoffer has a poster of Nobel Prize winners on the wall. One day Tommy answered a question and she got real excited. She went over to the poster and pointed to a spot.

"One day your picture will be here," she said. Of course it embarrassed Tommy, what kid wouldn't be embarrassed by such a thing? After class he made a joke about it. The next day somebody put Tommy's name next to the last winner. He laughed it off, but I believe it upset him.

He tries to be a regular guy. Actually, he's as goofy as the rest of the boys. Adults want to make him different. I saw a television special about Asian-American students. It suggested that they study harder and teachers think of them as smarter. According to the television reporter, both of these facts influence their grades. Tommy certainly studies harder than any kid I know. If it's really about studying, Tommy deserves his grades. But I've seen that other thing at work too.

One time last year we had a substitute. She was going around the room asking everybody a hard math problem. Finally, when she got bored with it, she turned to Tommy.

"I'm sure you know the answer," she said.

Tommy did know the answer; I knew it too. The point is, she didn't know anything about Tommy that she couldn't see. How did she know he knew the answer? For all she knew, Tommy could have been as dumb as spit. That's not fair to Tommy or the rest of us. Teachers expect so much from him that they never get to know the real Tommy M.

They never get to know that he has the worst case of allergies I've ever seen. From spring to late fall, Tommy is always just seconds from blowing his nose. Even right after a good blow, his voice has a snotty sound that's hard not to imitate sometimes.

We discovered there were four stores in the tri-county area that sold wheelchairs. I called the first two. The first man I talked to was real nice until I told him the wheelchair was for a classmate.

"How old is this child?" he asked.

"Twelve, but he's small for his age."

"We don't have anything that small," he said, and then he hung up.

"That was weird," I told Tommy. "That guy was pretty nice until I told him the chair was for a classmate."

"He probably thought you were an adult."

"So?"

"He probably figures you don't have the money. Your voice sounds older on the telephone. When you called yesterday, my mother thought you were a teacher."

"That's no reason to be so rude."

"Forget about it; it's his loss. Call the next number."

I dialed the next number on our list. This time I told the guy up front that I was checking on prices for a sixth-grade class project.

"He's twelve, but he's small for his age. . . . I don't know. . . . His name is Wayne. . . . I don't know. . . . Thank you." I hung up the phone.

"Why did he want to know his name?" Tommy asked.

"He said a twelve-year-old's parents were in yesterday to buy a motorized chair."

"Oh, what else did he ask?"

"He asked me what is his exact medical condition."

"I guess it would make sense to know all of

that. Maybe we can pay for a chair and they can measure Wayne for it later. They'll probably loan us a chair to use for the surprise."

"You think so?" I asked.

"Sure. People get real friendly when the sell is a sure thing. You didn't tell me how much it'll cost."

"I don't know yet. The guy said he would look up the prices and call me right back."

We were sitting in the kitchen. Three years ago my father built a wooden booth across one wall of our kitchen. One of his students helped. It seats about six adults, and it's the one thing everybody notices when they come into our house. It looks like something out of a magazine, it's so perfect. I believe my father is prouder of the breakfast nook than he is of his degrees. It's the only thing he's ever built. He doesn't tell people that the student who "helped" was his age and had worked for ten years as a carpenter before deciding he wanted to be a teacher.

"Do you want something to drink?" I asked Tommy.

"Yeah, and I wouldn't turn down a sandwich."

I made the sandwiches while Tommy poured us orange sodas. I had a mouthful of ham and cheese when the telephone rang.

"Yes, this is she. . . . Okay. . . . What? Is that the cheapest? . . . Okay, is that the most affordable? . . . All right, I'll tell my friends and we'll call you back."

"You don't look so good," Tommy said.

"You won't either when I tell you how much."

"I'm ready."

"Between one thousand and twenty-five hundred."

"No, seriously."

"I am serious."

"Maybe we can get a better price."

Tommy called the other two names on the list. My guy gave us the best range by about three hundred dollars.

"I guess there's nothing for us to do except tell the others. It's a good thing we didn't tell Wayne about it," I said.

Tommy finished his snack and we decided to play a video game before it was time for him to leave.

"What are you wearing to Faye's party?" he asked at the door. "I think it's a little silly for sixth-graders to dress up for Halloween, but it said on the invitation no costume, no admittance."

"I don't know yet," I told him. "Let's call a

meeting for after school to tell the others about the price."

"Okay, see you tomorrow."

I stood at the door in shock. Faye was having a party and she hadn't invited me! Tommy's words were the first I had heard about it.

I couldn't dial the twins' number fast enough. Mrs. Jenkins answered the telephone, and she wanted to talk about "long time, no see." I promised her I would visit soon, and she put Judge on the phone.

"Some friend you are," I said as soon as I heard Judge's voice.

"What are you talking about?"

"Faye's party."

"What about it?"

"Why didn't you tell me about it?"

"She didn't invite you?"

"No, she didn't invite me!"

Judge called Jury to the telephone. I heard him telling his brother what I had just told him.

"Did you two have a fight?" Jury asked.

"No, but she barely speaks to me anymore. I don't know why. We used to be pretty good friends."

"She's been acting real strange lately. Yesterday she told me I can bring a date to the party if I want."

"A date?" I repeated.

"Yeah, why would she say that?"

"I have no idea."

I heard Judge ask for the telephone. "Angela, we hadn't decided to go. Why don't the three of us go trick-or-treating like we used to?"

Good old Judge, always the peacemaker. "No, Judge, you guys go. It's no big deal." I know he heard my voice crack; I was on the verge of tears.

"I've got a better idea." It was Jury on the other line.

"What?" both Judge and I asked.

"Since Faye made a point of telling me I could bring a date, why don't you come as my date?"

"I can't date," I said, realizing it was a stupid thing to say as soon as I said it.

"I can't either, and I don't want to, and if I thought you'd think of it as a real date, I wouldn't go with you."

"Your parents won't think anything about us all going together. Last year was the first year since third grade that we weren't together on Halloween," Judge added.

"I don't know what Faye is up to, but it will blow her mind if you show up with us."

The thought of blowing Faye's mind brought a smile to my face.

"Okay, let's do it."

The next day we met with Miss Hoffer to tell

her about our progress. Standing next to Miss Hoffer's desk, it took everything I had not to let Faye know that I knew about her party.

"I guess we won't get to do it," Faye said, obviously disappointed.

"Don't be so sure," said Miss Hoffer. "I know some angels. How much of it can you guys raise?"

"It's too late to go through one of those fund-raising companies, but we called around and we found a candy distributor who will sell us candy canes at cost. Those big candy canes. It works out to be about two cents per candy cane and we can sell them for fifty cents," Jury said.

"How much profit is that?" Miss Hoffer asked.

Everybody looked at Tommy. He smiled. "We can make almost four hundred dollars if we use all of the money we have to buy candy canes."

"How many candy canes would we have to sell?"

"Seven hundred and fifty."

Everybody gasped.

"Don't get discouraged, that's not even one candy cane per student, and you don't have to limit your sell to the school," Miss Hoffer said.

"Right," I said. "We can sell them at the college too."

"I'm donating another fifteen dollars to buy candy canes. That will double our profit. And I'll talk to those angels about matching us."

I left the meeting charged. I felt good about what we were doing. As I walked home with Faye, the twins, and Tommy, I was thinking about volunteers. It was something to concentrate on so I wouldn't be tempted to tell Faye exactly what I thought about her. We all knew Miss Hoffer was talking about her church friends when she spoke of angels. They're always doing something for our class. One time we weren't going to be able to take a field trip because we couldn't get enough parents to volunteer to go with us. Miss Hoffer called on her angels, and three nice little old ladies saved the day. At the time I didn't think too much about it, but now I realized that volunteering must be its own reward. Two summers ago I told my mother I was too old to have a summer baby sitter. She told me it was either that or I had to go to work with her at the Community Center where she's the director. I volunteered in the day care center, but I resented it. I liked the kids and the staff, but I felt like they knew I was just avoiding the baby sitter.

When we got to Faye's turnoff, she had the nerve to say good-bye to me.

"I've never seen you so cold," Jury said. "I like that in a person." Judge laughed like an idiot.

"Why should I talk to her? She doesn't want to be my friend."

49

"There must be more to this," Judge said.

"What's going on?" Tommy finally asked.

The boys filled him in. He apologized for being the one to tell me about the party. "We've all known each other for a long time; I hope the old gang's not splitting up," Tommy said.

"It's just Faye; I think makeup has soaked into her brain."

"I knew it!" Tommy said. "I knew she was looking different lately."

"Do you wear makeup?" Judge asked me.

"No."

Jury patted me on the back. "It's worth a try, old girl."

He ran as I swung at him. The boys cracked up. I don't know if they were laughing at my attempt to hit Jury or at his crack on me.

That night I told my mother about the party. I told her I wanted to choose a really good costume.

"How about a gypsy," she suggested.

"Do they wear makeup?" I asked.

"I guess so, why?"

"I want to wear makeup."

"You're too young."

"Just for Halloween; I couldn't stand that stuff on my face every day."

"I wish I had a tape recording of you saying that so I can play it back in a few years."

"Come on, Mom, help me pick a good costume."

"I know! Cleopatra, that would take loads of makeup."

"What did she look like?" I asked. Unfortunately, my father was passing through the room at the time.

"Go look it up, baby. I'm sure I have several books on ancient Egypt in there. And you can try the encyclopedias too."

There were a lot of good pictures of what they thought she looked like. I especially liked her hairstyle because I knew it would be easy to copy. I showed my mother a picture and she volunteered to make me a dress.

"Can you have it ready by next Tuesday?" I asked.

"If we work together this weekend."

I just wish I had a video of the boys' faces when they picked me up on Halloween night. My mother told me repeatedly that I looked nice, and my father was very complimentary too. He made a half-hearted joke about not letting me go. But when I came out of the kitchen and Judge and Jury's mouths dropped open, I knew I had achieved the look I wanted.

My mother had stitched up a long tube out of a white sheet. She put elastic on one end to keep it from slipping off. Then she stitched a three-inch-wide, strange-looking, metallic lace gold collar all around the elastic neck. It was so tight that I split one side the first time I tried it on. She let it out a half inch on each side.

The boys knew my parents were watching for their reactions, so they didn't say anything until we were walking to Mrs. Jenkins's car.

"It's one thing to crash the girl's party, but you want to make her suffer, don't you?" Judge said.

"What do you mean?" I asked innocently as I batted the false eyelashes my mother had applied.

"Leave my date alone," Jury said. "If Faye can't stand the heat, she should've stayed out of the kitchen."

We laughed so hard, Judge warned me that I was going to split my dress.

"You kids might look different, but you sure sound the same," Mrs. Jenkins said when we couldn't stop giggling and Judge got the hiccups.

When I saw the boys, I thought they were dressed as twin Pee Wee Hermans, but it turned out they were the Blues Brothers. The only dark suits they owned were a size too small and they were waiting to put on the sunglasses later.

The drive over to Faye's took all of five minutes. We had it all planned. First Judge was to ring the doorbell, then Jury was supposed to step up behind him and mention that he had decided to bring a date after all. That would be my clue to step out from behind Jury.

As we approached Faye's house, I heard Jury say, "The best-laid plans of mice and men."

I was about to ask him what he meant when I noticed Faye standing in her driveway. She was bending over lighting a jack-o-lantern. She saw the car stop and waited for us to get out.

She didn't attempt to hide her confusion when she saw three kids get out. As we got closer and she saw it was me, she made even less effort to hide her anger. Jury said the words we rehearsed, but she was so busy checking me out, I doubt if she heard them.

"Angela, you look very nice."

"So do you, Faye."

She had on an ice skater's outfit. She did look nice, but she was no Cleopatra.

It was the best party I've ever attended. I haven't been to a lot of parties, but I think Faye's might rate up there with future parties. She went all out. She had just enough food, the right music, and a good mix of kids. About one third were older kids who had gone to Faber last year.

I know I should have felt guilty about having so much fun at a party I wasn't supposed to attend, but that just seemed to add to my enjoyment. The boys disappeared for long periods, but I didn't care. I danced three times with a seventh-grader named Desmond. When my father came to give us a ride home, Desmond told me he was looking forward to seeing me next year at the junior high school.

Faye walked us to the door. I think she was a little happier than she had expected to be. I saw Jury dancing with her twice.

"Angela, I'd like to stop by tomorrow, is that okay?" she asked me.

"My friends are always welcome at my house, Faye."

· *Chapter 7* ·

False Starts

One good thing about my school district, if Halloween falls on Monday through Thursday, the next day is always a teacher in-service day. I don't know if they do it for us or for the teachers and I don't care. It's nice not to have to go after being up so late.

My mother can't stand to see anybody sleeping when she's on her way to work. I used to think my father was kidding when he teased her about it, but lately I've noticed that she always manages to say something to me before she leaves. I don't mean "Good morning" or "Hi, honey"; she asks me questions that require me to be fully awake in order to answer. This morning she asked me to go downstairs and get her slip out of the dryer. When I saw the slip, I knew she had just wanted me out of bed. It was a half-slip and she could have put it on just before she walked out the door.

"Don't just sit around all day; you can start by cleaning up your room," she said when I handed her the slip.

"Okay. Can I go out?"

"Where?"

"I don't know, maybe the boys might want to do something."

"Has their mother gone back to work?"

"I don't think so."

"You can go over there if she's home, but I don't want kids in the house if I'm not here."

"Faye Benneck said she was going to come over."

"Oh, I haven't seen Faye around in quite a while." She paused to put on some lipstick. "Faye can come in, but just Faye — understand?"

"Got it."

She kissed me and got lipstick on my cheek. She thought it was funny when I tried to wipe it off.

"Be good."

"You know me," I said.

"That's why I said be good."

I went back to sleep for another ninety minutes. I probably would have slept longer, but hunger pains woke me.

I really like being in the house by myself. I fantasize that I'm an adult and I'm in my own home. Sometimes I'm independently wealthy and my money is somewhere working for me. Other times I'm a world-famous writer, actor, or consumer advocate and I'm working at home, but money is never the issue. Usually I put on a long silk robe that my mother is saving for something important. I float around the house in her robe dictating stuff to my imaginary secretary who is always male and bears a striking resemblance to my singer heartthrob of the moment. I was on my way to get the robe when Faye called.

"Angela, good morning."

Only Faye would say good morning as a greeting to another kid.

"Hi, Faye. Are you still coming over?"

"That's why I called. Is it all right?"

"Sure."

"In about an hour?"

"Okay."

I know I was supposed to ask her what this visit was about, but that would've seemed like I had a problem with her. I didn't. Whatever was going on was in her mind alone.

There was a time when Faye came to my house nearly every day. Before they moved to the "subdivide" she lived at the end of my block. She has two brothers who are in their twenties, so she's like an only child too. When my parents took me somewhere fun, I would ask Faye to come along. I've been places with her parents too. Last year her father had a mild stroke and her mother had to go back to work. My mother told me I should think of something to do for Faye's family. I decided I would help Faye with the housework so there would be one less thing for her mother to worry about. I went over to her house at least twice a week and we cleaned like a cleaning crew. Actually it was fun because we pretended we were a couple of android maids. We had the job down to seventy-five minutes, twice a week.

When Mr. Benneck recovered, he and Mrs. Benneck took me and Faye out to dinner at a real fancy restaurant. Also Mrs. Benneck wrote me a thank-you note and had it published on the "Our Kids" page of the local paper. That was kind of embarrassing. Neighborhood old ladies kept wanting to kiss me.

I got dressed and made my bed. I decided the best way to make it appear that I'd done some housework was to vacuum the living room. There's something about those lines the vacuum cleaner leaves that makes my mother think "clean."

I was standing in the living room when I saw Faye approach. Her hair was still sun-bleached from the summer. Usually her hair is a light brown, but in the summer it gets streaks of golden blond. I don't like the beauty salon streaks, but her natural streaks are nice. She still had her tan too. Faye likes her tan and so do I, but she complains all summer about the extra freckles that come with it. She's cute in that California-girl way. So far it hasn't gone to her head.

I answered the door on the first knock. She entered like it was her first visit to my home; it was strange. She looked around the room as if she expected to find hidden cameras.

"Are you okay?" I asked.

"Can I sit down?"

"Sure."

I knew I hadn't dreamed our past friendship when she walked past me and went to the kitchen. She sat down and I joined her.

"I'm sorry I didn't invite you to my party. It was wrong. You did so much for me when my father was sick and I acted like a brat."

I don't know if she paused because she wanted me to stop her, but I didn't.

"When I saw how much you enjoyed dancing with Desmond, I knew there was a chance that I was wrong."

"About what?"

"About you and Jury."

"What about us?"

"I thought you liked him."

"I do, he's my friend."

"You know what I mean."

"I guess I do know what you mean, but so what if I like him?" I asked.

"You do?"

"I didn't say that. I said, so what if I do?"

"I told Marsha Evans and Allie Fritz that I liked him and they have the biggest mouths in school. I know you've heard."

"Actually, I haven't, but I figured as much."

"Allie told Linn that you told Tommi Block that you didn't care about me, that he's your boyfriend."

"What? I haven't said more than three words to Tommi Block all year. And who is Linn?"

"He's in the other sixth grade. Allie likes him."

"Jury is my friend, period. I only went to your party with him because you didn't invite me."

"But he brought you, so he must like you. I just came over today because I want to be friends again."

"Jury brought me to the party because you didn't invite me. You've known Jury long enough to know helping me crash your party would be his idea of fun. I can't date, and if I could it wouldn't be Jury Jenkins."

"Would it be Judge?"

"No, I would look outside my family! I want us to be friends again too, but it sounds like we have different things on our minds."

"You don't think about boys?"

"Not any of these boys around here. Bobby Brown, Johnny Gill — yes. Jury Jenkins — never."

Faye laughed. My mentioning the two singers was the first time her face had cracked since she entered my house.

"Angela, that's not logical. You'll never even meet them."

"Oh, and it's logical for you to have a crush on a goofy boy who studies clichés and plays pompom tackle all the time. A boy you've known your entire life."

We both laughed. "I know it's silly, I don't know what's happening to me. Last month I had a crush on — are you ready for this?"

I nodded.

"I had a crush on Mr. C."

I screamed and felt her forehead. "You're a very sick child, Faye Benneck!"

"Tell me about it. My mother says my hormones have kicked in."

"What does that mean?"

"I guess grades are no longer the most important thing in my life."

"Does that mean that somebody else will actually have a crack at this year's first place in the science fair?"

"Don't count on it."

We laughed and talked for about another hour. When Faye went home, I felt that we were friends again.

The next day at school there was a rumor going around that Faye Benneck had come over to my house and beat me up for going to her party with Jury Jenkins. I don't know how it got started, but I do know that Faye must have told somebody she came to my house. I hadn't mentioned it to anybody.

As far as I was concerned, that was it. In the words of Jury, it was the straw that broke the camel's back. When a third-grader said, "I thought she broke your arm, where's the cast?" I didn't care if I ever spoke to Faye again.

I couldn't tell if Jury was embarrassed or flattered. We both acted like we hadn't heard the rumor, but he couldn't seem to stop grinning.

Faye had the nerve to have an attitude, like I was the one who went around telling everybody our business. After school we all met with Miss Hoffer. Faye wouldn't look at me. It was as if the day before hadn't happened.

"My mother is taking us to get the candy to-night," Judge told the group.

"Great, we can get started on Monday. Will we need permission to sell during recesses and lunch hours?" Tommy asked.

"I've already taken care of that," Miss Hoffer said. "We'll have a table set up on the west field. In addition to matching your profits up to five hundred dollars, my angels will work in the mall with you on Saturday. Also, I've made up these strips that I think we should attach to each candy cane."

The strips read: Thank you for supporting the Faber Elementary School Sixth Grade Christmas Project. The message was mimeographed about twenty times on a sheet of paper. It looked like she had about two hundred sheets.

"Who's going to cut all of those out?" Jury asked.

"I figured the class could do it tomorrow during art. And if you bring the candy tomorrow, we can start taping the thank you's on each cane."

I looked at Tommy, he looked at Jury. I'm sure we were all thinking the same thing: why bother?

"Can't we just tell everybody thank you when they buy the candy cane?" Jury asked.

"Oh, yes, I fully expect you guys to thank all of your buyers verbally, but I feel we need to identify our candy since we're selling something so common. Some enterprising young person could end up in business for him- or herself."

"It's going to take forever."

"Nonsense, the class will be able to cut the strips and attach them in less than an hour. Do you boys get a ride to school?" Miss Hoffer asked Judge.

"Unless it's raining, we walk."

"Then I'll stop by on my way in tomorrow; there's no need for you to carry all that candy. Now," she said, looking at me, "about the chair. How are things going?"

"We called the guy who gave us the best price. When we explained that we were trying to do this as a surprise, he said he would lend us a chair for the surprise, and Wayne could get fitted for his chair later."

"That's nice of him," Faye said.

"That's after we pay him for the chair," Tommy added.

"Oh."

"That sounds good. Now all we have to do is sell the candy," Miss Hoffer said with her usual cheerfulness.

Never in the history of candy-eating kids has there been such a sad start on a candy sale.

The sale began the following Monday. We had seven sells during the first recess, three during the second, and twenty-one during the two lunch periods.

"What's wrong?" Judge asked as we gathered up our stuff after the last lunch hour.

"I don't know," I said.

"A sudden interest in dental hygiene?" Tommy suggested.

"I'm surprised you don't know; I thought you knew everything!" Faye fired off at me.

"Do you know?" I asked, with as much anger as she was showing toward me. It was the first words we had spoken since that day at my house.

"I've got my ideas."

"Will you share them with us?" Tommy said in a teacher's voice. He was still trying to lighten up the mood.

"She should have realized that nobody would be that interested in buying candy this soon after Halloween!"

"If anybody should have had a firm fix on Halloween, it should have been you. I'm not the one who had a party."

"No, you're just the one who crashed it!"

"Ladies, please, we all made a mistake. Give it

time; by the end of the week sales should pick up," Judge said.

Jury patted him on the back. "Blessed be the peacemaker," he said to his brother.

Jury was the only one who laughed.

· Chapter 8 ·

Thanksgiving

Judge was right. As the kids finished off their Halloween stashes, they started buying our candy canes. By the Tuesday before Thanksgiving break, we had sold more than three hundred dollars' worth. We were all banking on the Friday after Thanksgiving, the busiest shopping day of the year, and we had permission to sell in the mall.

Things were the same between me and Faye. I noticed that she looked for my name on the mall sign-up sheet. Apparently she didn't want to work the same time as me, and that's the way I would have planned it too.

Thanksgiving is my favorite holiday. I like Christmas, but the vacation gets a bit too long and sometimes it's too cold in December. Thanksgiving time is perfect. I like to spend as much time as possible on campus with my father

67

because the trees around his building are beautiful. When I was a little girl, I thought it looked like Oz.

My mother misses her big family during the holidays, so she always invites as many friends as possible to eat with us. This year she invited two single mothers she works with. It's a good thing I like little kids so much because the two women have five kids between them.

Thanksgiving dinner was great. I didn't mind eating at the kids' table because the kids were so much fun. It was flattering the way they tried to imitate everything I did.

After dinner, Judge and Jury came over and taught the kids how to play pom-pom tackle. When the guests left, the twins and I went to see a movie. It was the same thing we did last year, but with everything that was happening, I didn't expect to see them this year.

It was a wonderful day. Judge and Jury were no different than they were when we were seven and all had the chicken pox together. Their mother stayed with us for two days and then my mother stayed with us for two days. Except for the itching, it was the most fun I've ever had.

Thanksgiving was well on its way to being one of those memorable moments until the movie ended. We were in the lobby of the theater getting our walking-home box of popcorn when we met Faye and two of her friends. I wasn't surprised by her attitude. It was the boys who surprised me. We had been laughing and playing until Judge spotted Faye.

"There's your girl," he said to me.

I looked to see who he was talking about, turned around, and was almost face to face with Faye, Tommi, and another girl I didn't recognize.

"Well, look who's here," she said, looking directly at Jury.

"Hi Faye, Tommi, and I don't know your name," Jury said to the stranger.

"This is my cousin Kathy, she lives in Lexington. Kathy, these are my dear friends, Jury and Judge Jenkins, and that's Angela Collins."

"Hi, I've heard a lot about you guys."

Jury looked at me and grinned. As cute as Faye is, cousin Kathy looked like the "after" side to Faye's "before." She was about fourteen. She had Faye's long hair, but hers was even more sunbleached. The freckles that Faye gets all over her face were confined to Kathy's nose. Kathy's tan was a little deeper than Faye's. The most striking difference was the two extra inches in height and the two extra inches on her bustline and hips. I noticed that passers-by stared in appreciation at cousin Kathy.

"Are you coming or going?" Judge asked.

"We're just getting here," Faye said.

"You'll like the movie, it's as good as the hype," Jury said. I noticed he looked at cousin Kathy as he spoke.

"We better go so we can get good seats. I guess I'll see you guys tomorrow at the mall."

"Is your cousin coming with you?" Jury asked.

"No, I'm leaving in the morning, but we're thinking about coming down for Christmas. Maybe I'll see you again then."

"Yeah, maybe Faye will have another one of those great parties," Jury said.

Faye grinned from ear to ear. I'm sure she had told her cousin about her party, but to have Jury confirm that it was a great party must have made her feel like a queen.

I couldn't believe how the boys were acting. In a split second, they went from two pom-pom-tackle-playing boobs to sophisticated gentlemen. All in the presence of a pretty girl.

We walked out of the theater. As soon as we got outside in front of the theater, they looked at each other, laughed, and gave each other high fives.

"What's that all about?" I asked.

They looked at each other and repeated the high fives.

"Did I miss something?" I asked.

Judge saw that I was getting upset. "We're just being silly. It's not about you."

I knew it wasn't about me and that's why I was upset. I was jealous. Jealous of cousin Kathy and all the girls who'll make the boys slap palms in the future.

I had the eleven-to-one-o'clock shift selling candy. Tommy and Miss Hoffer worked with me, and it was interesting to sit in the mall and watch all the different types pass by. We compared different people to animals and that was fun for a while. But I had other things on my mind. I couldn't get the movie incident out of my mind.

"Tommy, when you see an attractive woman or girl, will you point her out to me?"

"Why?"

"I just want to know what boys consider cute."

"See that girl right there, the one with the black jeans? She's cute, but her mother or whoever that women with her is, is pretty."

I looked at the two women. The girl was probably in her late teens and the other woman was probably in her late thirties. They were white, the woman had deep auburn hair, the girl brown hair. They weren't close enough for me to see their faces, so I couldn't understand how Tommy could call them attractive.

"How can you say that when they're not close enough to see what they look like?"

He blew his nose. "I noticed them when they passed."

"So you look at girls?"

"Of course."

"Are the ones you look at always white?"

"No, I've seen attractive girls of all races today. See this woman coming toward us. The one with the cotton candy?"

I looked in the direction of his nodding head. The woman was black. She was average height with medium-brown skin. She was cute in a news-anchorwoman kind of way. Not striking, but attractive. I was afraid that Tommy misunderstood what I wanted from him. I wasn't trying to make a political statement, I really wanted to know — what is cute?

"Tommy, she doesn't have to be black. Just point out any woman you think looks attractive."

"I really think that woman is attractive. Lately, on that rare occasion when a Japanese girl comes on the television, my parents go on and on about how pretty she is. Sometimes the girl isn't pretty, just Japanese. I think they're afraid that I'm not attracted to my own people. They're talking about sending me to visit relatives in Japan this summer. I would love to go to Japan, but not just to scout Japanese babes."

"Do you think you'll marry a Japanese girl?"

"Yes, I think I will, but I think it will be for the same reason most people marry within their race. Whatever that reason is."

"Suppose you meet a girl who's not Japanese and you have a lot in common. You both like the same things and the same kind of people."

"Then that's probably the girl I'll marry. Why all the questions? Are you looking for a husband?"

"No." I laughed. "I'm just trying to understand things." We had this conversation between candy sales. It's a good thing Miss Hoffer knows nearly everybody in town. She was so busy talking to passers-by that she didn't pay any attention to us.

My two hours went fast. There was no doubt in my mind that we would sell all the candy canes.

"I just spotted a woman that I think is really pretty. I know this woman and I've always thought so," Tommy whispered to me.

I looked where he was looking and saw my mother. I nudged Tommy with my knee and he laughed.

"I'm serious."

I had enough problems without worrying

about what my friends think of my mother's looks.

I walked around the mall with my mother. She loves to shop and she likes my taste in clothes. We shop well together.

On our way to the car, we stopped by the candy table. Jury was working with Faye. I don't know how she pulled that off, because I know he signed up to work with his brother.

"How're sales?" my mother asked.

"I doubt if we have enough candy to last another hour," the always-polite Faye volunteered.

"Did you guys enjoy the movie?" my mother asked Jury.

"It was good; you should've seen the car crashes."

"I'll pass. Take care, kids."

"I noticed you didn't have much to say," my mother said once we were in the car.

"How could I have gotten a word in?"

She smiled, but I had a feeling that she knew there was more to it.

· Chapter 9 ·

Details

On Monday, Faye announced to the class that we were twenty dollars over our goal. The class didn't know this, but that meant we had raised at least five hundred and twenty dollars. It was her job to downplay our project. The class believed what they were told, that the money would be used to benefit a family in our neighborhood. For the most part, they didn't care. They would have been much more enthusiastic if they had known that the money was for Wayne's motorized wheelchair, but there's no way they could have kept the secret.

After school our group had a brief meeting. Miss Hoffer told us she would take the money and her group's check to the medical supply store that evening. The only thing left to do was to figure out when we were going to present Wayne with the chair.

"Why don't we do it during our regular Christmas party?" Judge suggested.

"I thought we would do it during the Christmas assembly next week," Miss Hoffer said.

"I know Wayne; that would be too embarrassing for him," I said, and surprisingly, Faye agreed.

"They're right. It'll be hard enough for Wayne to accept it with just our class there," Tommy said.

"We could just have it delivered to his house. Why do we have to be there? We know he's going to appreciate it."

"Oh Jury, what was the point of keeping it a secret if that's all we're going to do?"

"What's your idea, Faye!"

"Calm down, we'll come up with something," Miss Hoffer said.

This was an interesting change. Faye was talking to Jury in the same tone she used when he took her sweater as a pom-pom.

"Is anybody in class having a Christmas party?" Tommy asked.

"I haven't heard anything, but sometimes I don't," I said. I don't know why I said it; it was a mean crack. Faye turned beet-red. Jury laughed aloud. She glared at him.

"Why, would a house party be better?" Judge asked.

"Not necessarily a house party, but something away from school. Do you think your mother would let us use the center?"

"That's a great idea. Will you ask her, Angela?" Faye asked. I could tell that something was different with her. She was trying to be nice to me, and she was doing it in a natural way as if nothing had happened.

"Sure, it's the community's center. If there's nothing on the calendar, she'll let us schedule a party. We'll need to give her a date."

Miss Hoffer looked at a calendar on the wall behind her. It's a wonder she could remember it was back there with all her junk on the wall.

"How about next Friday?"

"Okay, I'll tell her, Friday the thirteenth." We all looked at each other.

My father was waiting for me when I walked out of school. I was a little sorry to see him because I thought I noticed something interesting happening between Jury and Faye. They seemed to be arguing about every little thing.

"Do you want to run with me? I brought your shoes."

"Okay, but I've probably only got one lap in me."

"Are you having one of those days too?"

"I've had better." Before I could tell him about all the little things happening in my life, my father started telling me about his job. He was worried about cutbacks on campus. His job wasn't being threatened, but the people who make his job easier were being laid off. He was down to one teaching assistant.

"Daddy, I can come in on Saturdays and make copies and stuff for you," I offered. "Have you thought about computer-scored tests?"

"I prefer essay tests. English doesn't lend itself well to computerized tests. But I appreciate the suggestion and the offer. Don't worry about me; I'm just sounding off a little. Tell me what's happening in your life."

As we jogged around the track, I brought my father up to date on Project Wheels. He laughed so hard he had to stop running.

"What's so funny?"

"It's not funny, it's wonderful. You have the life I prayed for on the day you were born. From what you've told me, you're not worried about whether or not you'll have food on your table tonight and your clothes don't seem to be falling apart."

"You're making fun of me."

He wrapped his arm around me. "No, I'm not. I'm happy for you. You have good friends, a caring teacher, and parents who love you. Enjoy your life and stop worrying. Wayne will like the chair, Jury and Faye will stop arguing, and next week it'll be something else that seems just as important."

Miss Hoffer was absent on Tuesday. It was the second time she had missed since school began in August. When she didn't come in on Wednesday, we got worried. Finally Faye had the idea to talk to Mrs. Keats.

"Miss Hoffer has to call in when she's sick, and she probably talks to Mrs. Keats."

During recess Faye, Tommy, and I went to the office to ask Mrs. Keats what was happening to our teacher.

"Why? Is there a problem with the substitute?" she asked Faye. I noticed she wouldn't make eye contact with me or Tommy.

"We're working on a project and we need her," I said before Faye could answer. I wanted to see if she would talk to me.

"She has the flu, so she'll probably be out the rest of the week," she said to Faye. "Now, you kids get back out to recess."

"That was weird," Faye said.

"No, it wasn't," Tommy told her. "She always acts like that."

79

"She's always nice to me."

"No kidding," I said, and Tommy and I laughed.

"Are you guys saying she's prejudiced?"

"I'm saying the way she acted today is the way she has treated me since I first stepped foot in that office," I said.

"Do you realize that in six years she has never called my father Dr. Masaki. Even if he calls and says, 'Hello, this is Dr. Masaki,' she'll say, 'Yes, Mr. Masaki.' You tell us, Faye, what is that?"

"It's sad, that's what it is."

Then the oddest thing happened. I saw Faye changing toward Tommy. She started asking him a lot of questions, and she was hanging on every word he said. I left them talking on the side of the school while I stood in line to play four square. I could see them from where I played; they stood there talking until the bell rang. I'm sure Tommy didn't know that Faye was targeting him for her next crush. He thought he was having an innocent conversation with a friend.

After school we met in the library. By then everybody knew that Miss Hoffer was going to be out for the rest of the week.

"What do you guys think we should do?" Faye asked.

"There's nothing we can do but wait," Jury answered. "What do you think we should do, call her up and tell her she better get back to school?"

"I would expect that from you! I'm asking the group if they feel we should postpone the party."

"I don't think so. We can plan the details. Tomorrow we can send around a sign-up sheet for refreshments, and there's a good built-in sound system at the center, so all we need is albums or cassettes," I said. "And decorations."

"Why don't we work on decorations, Tommy?" Faye asked.

Tommy jerked as if Faye's words had struck the side of his face. "Okay. That sounds okay."

"Let's make a list of all the music we have between the five of us," Judge suggested.

"Don't worry about the music; I have everything from the party," Faye said.

When Miss Hoffer came back to school on Monday, we learned that she still hadn't contacted the man about the chair. Apparently she'd gotten sick after school on the evening she'd planned to take the money to him. She still hadn't fully recovered and was glad that we'd gone ahead with the details.

"I'll go call him now; this should only take a minute."

When she left the room, Faye and Jury started

arguing about who knows what, I started my homework assignment, and Judge and Tommy played tic-tac-toe.

Miss Hoffer didn't look too good when she left the room. When she came back, she looked even worse.

"Is something wrong, Miss Hoffer?" Faye asked.

"Gather around, guys — we've got a problem."

· Chapter 10 ·

Setback

"I talked to the man at the store. He gave me the same price range he gave you. He said we can buy a good model for one thousand dollars —"

"That's what he told us," Tommy interrupted.

"But that figure includes a three-hundred-dollar trade-in on his old wheelchair!"

"What!" I said.

"He didn't say anything about that!"

"Oh no, I can't believe this is happening to us." Faye was on the verge of tears.

"Okay, let's calm down and think this thing through. At the very worst, we'll have to tell Wayne about the surprise. He'll still get his chair," Miss Hoffer said.

"Did the guy at the store say anything about being willing to wait for the trade-in?" Tommy asked.

"I asked him about that, but he said he wasn't

the owner and he was already overstepping his limits on the deal he quoted to you."

"Do you believe him?" Jury asked.

"He did give us the best prices," I said.

"We've just got to figure out a way to get the chair away from Wayne," Judge said.

Everybody looked at him. I didn't know what the others were thinking, but I figured it would be easier to take a cub from a mother lion than to get Wayne's wheelchair from him without telling him why.

It was cold out when we left the school. I was still wearing my summer windbreaker, but I knew that wouldn't be the case for long. Miss Hoffer had given us the task of figuring out a way to get the chair from Wayne, take it to the store, and replace it with the motorized chair. All during the course of a two-hour party.

We were all walking together until Faye turned off. The boys were playing catch with Jury's baseball cap. As soon as Faye turned off, I heard Tommy tell the twins, "I need to talk to Angela for a minute." He fell back in step with me.

"Remember that strange conversation we had in the mall?" he asked.

"Why animals look like people?"

"No, about beauty and girls, that stuff?"

"Yeah, I remember."

"Were you trying to tell me something?"

"No, I told you then, I really wanted to know what boys consider attractive. Why?"

"Angela, Faye has been acting real weird lately. Remember that day we went to the office to talk to Mrs. Keats?"

"Uh huh."

"Ever since that day, she's been following me around and calling me."

"What does she say?"

"She'll ask for the math assignment or for the spelling words. But you know Faye doesn't need any help. Her grades are as good as mine. Most of the time she doesn't even take her backpack home because she finishes her homework in class."

"It sounds like she likes you."

"What am I supposed to do about it?"

"What do you want to do about it?"

We came to the corner that was Tommy's turn-off. We stopped walking. I noticed that the twins were going on ahead, meaning that I would have two blocks to walk alone.

"I want us to continue being friends. You see what happened when she stopped liking Jury."

"Yeah, they fight like cats and dogs. Forget I said that, I'm beginning to sound like him."

"When I think about going to junior high next year, I get scared."

"So do I," I admitted.

"But then I remember that I have two cool twin brothers who are my friends and two great-looking, smart girls who are my friends and I don't feel so scared."

I didn't know what to say. When I was asking Tommy to comment on girls, I purposely didn't ask about myself because I figured he had never considered my looks.

"It really bothered me when you and Faye were fighting."

"We never actually fought. That was just a rumor."

"I know, but when the two of you weren't as close anymore. Angela, I want you to tell Faye not to like me. I just want to be friends."

"Oh Tommy, why me? We just got back on speaking terms."

"Because she'll listen to you."

I didn't say anything. The boys reached their turnoff and hollered good-bye to us. Tommy and I waved. Poor Tommy, standing outside was driving his allergies crazy. His eyes were watering and his voice was especially snotty.

"Will you do it?"

"Okay, I'll call her tonight." I started walking.

"If you come up with an idea for Project Wheels, call me."

"Okay, 'bye. Thanks, Angela."

As I walked the rest of the way by myself, I thought about the fact that nobody calls me Angie. I've always wanted a nickname and I've got a perfect tie-in for one, but nobody uses it. I tried not to think about what Tommy had asked me to do. And the last thing I wanted to think about was how we were going to get that chair from Wayne.

The house was empty when I got home, but it's usually that way after school. So first I called my mother because she wants me to let her know when I get home.

"Are you busy?" I asked her.

"No more than usual. Why, baby, what's wrong?"

"Nothing is really wrong, but we've got a problem with the wheelchair."

"What?"

"The price the man told us for the new chair included a trade-in."

"And?"

"And how are we going to keep it a surprise if we have to get the old chair from Wayne?"

"Do his parents know about the surprise?"

"No, we figured we would surprise them too. Actually, there was some talk about whether or not Mr. DeVoe would be too proud to take it if he knew in advance. Remember how he acted when they had a fire and the PTA donated those boxes of clothes?"

"Yes, I do remember. I'm sure you guys will come up with something. Let me know if I can help."

"Okay, 'bye."

"Angela, take something out for dinner."

"All right, 'bye."

She had more confidence in our ability to work things out than I had. I went into the kitchen and took out a frozen hunk of meat. I couldn't tell what it was, but my mother didn't tell me to identify it. She just said to take it out.

I decided to call Faye before doing my homework. My father always tells me to do the hardest thing first; that way the rest of your tasks seem easy. I had to do my homework, clean my room, empty the dishwasher, and call Faye. Calling Faye was by far the hardest.

I dialed her number by memory. I hung up before the first ring and decided I would make a list of all the numbers I knew by heart.

"No, I'm just trying to waste time," I said as I dialed again. "Hello, Faye, are you busy?"

"Not really. Have you figured out how we're going to do it?"

"No, I'm calling about something else. I talked to Tommy on the way home from school."

"Oh."

I thought about something Jury had said about catching more flies with honey, and I realized I should change my approach.

"Faye, we've all been friends for a long time."

"Uh huh."

I could tell she was being careful with her answers. I shouldn't have said I talked to Tommy first. "When you think about it, there's not many kids other than the five of us who have been in all the same classes since kindergarten."

"That's true. What were you and Tommy talking about?"

"He said that when he thinks about going to junior high, he gets scared and I told him I do too. Does it scare you, Faye?"

"It excites me more than it scares me. Remember how we used to sit around the quad looking at the college kids?"

"Sure."

"Well, college was okay to think about, but it always seemed like a little too much work. When I looked at my brothers, they were the ones who seemed to have so much fun. They were in their early teens around that time. Why does it scare you?"

"There will be so many kids there that we don't know."

"That's true."

"Tommy was saying it helps him to remember that he has me and you and the twins. He doesn't want to see anything interfere with our friendships. It bothered him when you and I weren't speaking."

"It did?"

"Yeah, it did."

"Did he ask you to talk to me?"

"Yes," I admitted.

"I guess he knows that I've developed a crush on him?"

"Uh huh."

"And he wants me to leave him alone?"

"No, he wants you to continue to be his friend. He's afraid the same thing that happened to you and Jury will happen to the two of you."

"I understand," she said. I could hear the hurt in her voice.

"Faye, I'm sorry."

"Don't be. He's right, both of you are. Let's make a pact. From now on we're a posse, one for all and all for one."

"Sounds good to me. Call me if you figure out something."

"Okay, 'bye."

"'Bye."

I went upstairs and cleaned my room. A posse, I liked that. Now all I had to worry about was how to get that chair from Wayne.

· Chapter 11 ·

The Party

The idea came to me at three o'clock in the morning. I wasn't awake and worrying about it. In fact, I was dreaming about Faye. Since our friendship was slowly starting to rebuild itself, I'd been thinking about her a lot. I guess I'd come to realize that if Judge and Jury are the brothers I've never had, Faye is the sister. And sometimes sisters fight.

Anyway, I was dreaming about Faye. It was something about us running from a yappy little dog — I don't remember the details. I was sound asleep and I bolted straight up in the bed. It was so simple. I wished I could call everybody right then to tell them.

I was tired when the alarm clock rang three hours later. I'm a person who needs no less than a solid five-hour block of sleep if I'm going to feel rested. Also, my throat had an odd feeling, not that it hurt, but it felt the way it feels the day after I scream too much at a football game.

I dragged myself out of bed. The room was cold. My mother has a fondness for hardwood floors, but on mornings like this I wish I had carpet.

I could hear my parents talking. They're morning people. I'm a midmorning, late afternoon person. From about ten to two, and after six at night but before eleven, I'm your girl. Any hours in between, leave me alone. I don't know why, but every day at about quarter to three I get so sleepy I want to stretch out on the classroom floor. When we studied the Latin American countries and learned about siestas, I knew I wasn't alone. Most days I don't get to take one, but when I do I'm a better person for it.

"Good morning," my father said when we passed in the hallway. "Have you figured out anything about the chair?"

"I sure did. I'll discuss it with the group this morning."

"Does that mean I have to wait to hear about it?"

"Just until this evening."

"All right."

I have GATE class with Faye and Tommy, but I don't see the twins until we go to our regular classroom. Surprisingly, they were playing pom-pom tackle before school. I decided to wait until we could all get together.

It was finally cold enough for my corduroy skirt. Most of the leaves were gone from the trees, and it was starting to look like Christmas. Pretty soon the campus would be deserted and my father would be grading finals. Not long after that, relatives from Milwaukee or Decatur or both would be arriving and things would begin to get real busy and weird.

Miss Hoffer was back to her old self. I suspect that Christmas is a good time for her. Last year she had so many decorations up she even decorated the outside of her classroom door. My cousins from Milwaukee always say it's too warm in Kentucky for a "real" Christmas, and my cousins from Georgia say it's too cold. I figure they're all crazy. Kentucky Christmases are perfect.

After GATE I went to talk to Miss Hoffer. "I've got a plan," I told her. "I think it will work, but it'll put us on a tight schedule during the party."

"Okay, Angela, let's hear it."

I told her. After school we told the group, and everybody agreed that it just might work.

The day went fast. Usually when you're this close to a vacation everything moves really slow.

I went over to Faye's after school because she had asked me to help her make decorations for the party. Tommy was supposed to be sharing the job with her, but she thought it best not to ask him. She had a lot of red and green construction paper, and we made those paper strip chains from kindergarten. We cut out some Christmas trees and some stars too.

Most of our conversation centered around school gossip. She didn't bring up Jury or Tommy and until it was time for me to leave, I forgot about them.

"Did you tell Tommy we talked?" Faye asked when I said that I had to leave.

"Yeah, I told him."

"What did he say?"

"All he said was, 'That's good. In a little while everything should be back to normal.'"

She tried to smile, but I could see it wasn't easy. I couldn't help but wonder when life had become so serious for her. I suspect it had something to do with her father getting sick last year. My parents are younger than hers and they've always been healthy. But when her father got sick, it made me think about my parents dying and for days I couldn't sleep. It was scary.

"When my brothers were teenagers, I was just starting school," Faye announced, out of the blue as far as I could tell. "They're just a year apart so they have lots of the same friends."

"Uh huh."

She smiled at me. I guess she could see that I thought her statements were a little strange.

"My oldest brother was actually pretty shy. He figured out that girls thought it was cute when he took me places, and they would come up to him to talk about me or play with me. I got to go everywhere, games, movies, you name it. Whenever girls came over to the house, I got to sit on his lap for the first few minutes."

"I remember. I used to wish they were my brothers. When you guys moved I was afraid they would forget me."

"I didn't figure out why he used to keep me around so much until last year. But it didn't matter because I loved it. I've always thought being a teenager was the most fun time in a person's life. From the time I was five, I've been living for the day that I could have the kind of fun my brothers used to have. Maybe I've been rushing it."

I didn't say anything. What was there to say?

The next two days were so typical that I could have forgotten about the party. Winter had arrived. My long trench coat wasn't warm enough on the walk to school. Everybody was complaining about the weather.

"It's going to be a rough winter, I can tell," my mother said as she offered me a ride to school. I didn't take a ride, but I agreed with her about winter. I don't dread winter as much as she does. It's not my favorite time, but I don't hibernate.

My GATE teacher was out Friday and Mr. C. taught the class. GATE is usually very relaxed, but Mr. C. changed the atmosphere. He turned it into a real class, so it wasn't much fun. And Miss Hoffer seemed to have something upsetting on her mind during social studies. We were studying European history, so I'm pretty sure it wasn't the subject.

I noticed that three kids were out with the flu that was going around. I wasn't feeling too good myself.

Glancing around the room, I noticed that Judge and Jury had new haircuts. Their uncle is a barber and their hair always looks nice. I looked at Faye. Her head was buried in her backpack. She and Tommy had been laughing together after GATE; that was a good sign. I think they'd been avoiding each other since the day I called her.

Everybody at school was talking about the party. For some reason, the kids had the idea that the party was going to be wilder than usual because it wasn't being held at school. If anything, it would be tamer.

As fast as the rest of the week went, Friday was

the longest day I'd had in a while. I thought I would scream when Miss Hoffer finally said, "I guess I'll see all of you later at the party."

The party was scheduled for five o'clock. I had to be there at three to help the guys with the food and the decorations.

I had ridden my bike to school because I knew I'd be in a hurry. Jury tried to get me to give him a ride, but I'd promised my parents I wouldn't ride two to a bike. Anyway, that would have left Judge to walk by himself.

At home I changed into my party clothes and packed the stuff I needed for the surprise. So much depended on Wayne acting according to plan. I hoped he was going to be in one of his cooperative moods.

I called my mother to let her know that I was on my way over to the center. She was in a meeting, but the receptionist took the message. Just before I left the house, I called my father to make sure he hadn't forgotten his role in the plan. He was teaching, but somebody in his office took the message.

The center is about four miles from my house. It's only five minutes away by car, but it takes me fifteen minutes on my bike. I rode past the campus. It was too cold to student-watch because they were moving too fast.

By the time I got to the center, I was feeling sick to my stomach. It wasn't nerves or something I ate; it was the flu. There was no doubt in my mind. I refused to give in to it.

"Not now," I whispered to myself. "After the party." I couldn't help but wonder if I was the only kid in the world who gets sick just before the really big events in her life.

Faye was already there. I spotted her right away. She was on a stepladder hanging the Merry Christmas sign.

"Is this a good place, Angela?" she called out to me.

"Perfect," I said. As soon as the words came out I felt my lunch trying to follow. I ran past the twins and my mother to the restroom.

"I knew it!" my mother said as she ran in behind me. "That's why I tried to give you a ride this morning. I knew something was wrong with you. I'll have the boys put your bike in the car and I'll take you home."

"Mama, please, I've worked so hard on this." I started crying, not because I didn't feel I could convince her to let me stay but because I felt really bad.

"Tell me where it hurts."

"My stomach and my head."

"I've got some medicine in my desk that should

get you through the party, but I want you to lie down for about an hour."

"But the decorations . . ."

"They can put up those decorations without you."

"I have to tell Daddy . . ."

"Everybody knows what to do; you come with me. I'll put you on a cot until the other kids start to arrive."

I knew it was useless to argue. I went with her to the office and took three tablespoons of pink medicine and a tablet for the headache. She dragged in a cot from the day care center. It just wasn't fair. Here we were about to see two months' worth of hard work pay off and I get the flu. And it was coming at a time when it would only interfere with vacation time. It wasn't fair.

"Go to sleep."

I didn't expect to fall asleep. It was so noisy in the hall that I didn't think I could. The last thing I remembered was somebody, it sounded like Jury, playing disc jockey on the sound system.

"Angela, Angela."

I opened my eyes to see my mother. The headache was gone and my stomach felt less mad.

"Honey, the kids are starting to come. Wayne is here."

"Is Daddy here?"

"The boys said he just pulled up. How do you feel?"

"Better, but I'm not making any plans for the weekend."

"Good choice. Let's go greet your public."

The kids had done an excellent job with the decorations. The food table looked good too, but my stomach told me not to stand too close to it. I noticed that the "angels" were present. I imagine they had something to do with all the pretty cakes and cookies I saw.

Miss Hoffer looked happier than she had earlier. "Feeling better, Angela?"

"A little."

"There's not much you can do about it but get plenty of rest and fluids."

"All right."

She seemed to want to say something else. I waited.

"I finally convinced Wayne's father to go along with everything about twenty minutes ago," she confessed.

She saw the shock on my face and laughed. We knew she had been working on convincing Wayne's father to let him accept our gift, but since she hadn't mentioned it, I figured everything was fine in that department.

"He can be as difficult as his son."

"How did you do it?" I asked.

"I prayed on it, but it was his wife who finally convinced him. We had been telling him right along that he owed it to his son, regardless of how he felt about it, but somehow she was able to hit the right nerve."

"I'm glad she did."

"We saved Wayne for you," Faye said as she walked up.

"Is he in a good mood?"

"With Wayne, who knows?"

I walked over to where Wayne was talking with two boys from my class. I greeted all three of them.

"Wayne, could I ask you a favor?"

"You can ask, but before you do, let me ask you something. Why did everybody on your stupid committee ask me if I was planning to come today?"

"Oh, that's because of the favor I want to ask."

"Okay, what do you want?"

"Do you see that table over there?" I pointed to a table in the corner.

"I'm crippled, not blind! What about it?"

"Will you work it?"

"What do you mean work it?"

102

"We're setting the party up as kind of a Las Vegas night. All the floor space out here will be devoted to dancing. All the tables against the wall will be devoted to games . . ."

"And you guys figured that since I'm not dancing, I can work a table."

"Did you plan to dance, Wayne?"

He started laughing. He knows he can't pull that mess with me because I'll throw it right back.

"I might have some socializing to do."

"This is Angela, Wayne. Since when did you start socializing?"

"What did you think I was doing when you so rudely interrupted me?"

"Boring those two boys."

We both laughed. I started pushing him over to the table set up for him.

When we reached the table we found that it was too short for his chair to fit comfortably underneath. As luck and planning would have it, my father stepped up.

"Can I help?"

"You can find us a higher table, Mr. Collins," Wayne said. It was so like Wayne to suggest a higher table rather than the plan we had set up.

"There aren't any more tables. What are we going to do?" I asked, probably a bit too dramatically.

"I can help Wayne get on the chair that's already there. How does that sound to you, Wayne?"

Wayne looked at the chair like we were asking him to buy it. It was my mother's desk chair, the best chair in the building. Wayne looked around the room to see if anybody was watching him. One of our most important instructions was not to look at the table until I stepped away from it. There's no way Wayne would allow my father to lift him from his chair if anybody was looking.

Jury had created a crowd of kids watching him do a magic trick. Absolutely nobody was looking in our direction.

"It looks like a comfortable chair. I guess that will be okay," Wayne said.

My father quickly lifted him from his wheelchair and into the chair behind the table.

"Let me see where you're putting my chair."

"Right here, against the wall next to you."

I showed Wayne the game he was supposed to be playing with the kids and walked away from the table.

Judge gave me a high five when I walked over to the crowd of kids watching Jury.

"Now lower the lights and create a crowd around Wayne's table." Judge left to do as I asked.

I saw my father take the chair, but I knew to watch. Wayne was having so much fun doling out the mad money we were using for our game tables that he didn't see it.

Just as I suspected, there was very little dancing. At Faye's party, the older kids got the dancing started. We had invited the other sixth grade, but the boys in that class weren't any more likely to ask a girl to dance than the ones in my class.

Wayne freaked when his parents walked in. They came a little earlier than expected; we had told them we were presenting him with the chair early in the party. I was standing by his table when they walked in.

"Angela, my parents are here! Something must be wrong." he said, immediately looking for his wheelchair. I imagined he figured he would be leaving. "My chair!"

"What?" I said.

"It's gone, my chair is gone." He was as close to tearful as I've ever seen him. "Who would take my chair?"

A crowd of kids gathered around the table. They didn't know the plan, and they began to look around the hall and to sympathize with him.

"This is the cruelest thing I have ever seen," one girl said and began to cry.

"Calm down, we'll find it," Miss Hoffer said.

"It shouldn't be lost! Mr. Collins put it right there," Wayne said, pointing to the wall. "Where is your father, Angela?"

"Are you accusing my father of stealing your chair, Wayne?"

"No, dear, he's not saying that. He wants to ask your dad about it," Mrs. DeVoe said. She was so convincing in her concern I wondered if she realized this was all part of the plan.

I was starting to get a little worried until the house lights came back on.

"Finally, some light," somebody said.

"Now we can really look around."

"Can I have everybody's attention?" It was Faye on the microphone. "Wayne DeVoe's wheelchair is missing . . ."

"Yes it is!" Wayne shouted out.

"And the reason it is missing is because his sixth-grade class decided he didn't need it anymore."

"What is she talking about?" Wayne said, almost to himself.

"He doesn't need it anymore because of this . . ." Faye pointed to the doorway closest to Wayne, and Jury came riding in on the new chair.

There was stunned silence in the room.

Tommy was walking behind Jury with a huge card. The card must have been his idea, or one they came up with while I was asleep.

It took a moment or two for the reality to soak in.

"Is it mine?" Wayne asked me.

"It's all yours. Merry Christmas!"

Wayne fought back the tears, but his mother made up for him. She cried enough for two people. Mr. DeVoe's back was stiff with pride as he moved closer. He helped Wayne into the chair, and Wayne was all over the place with it.

"Are you ready to go hit the sheets?" my mother asked.

"I'm feeling better; can't I stay until the end?"

She looked around the room. Wayne was still rolling around demonstrating his chair. His parents were watching him. His mother was still wiping away tears and his father was smiling

Some of the kids had finally started dancing. Faye, Tommy, Judge, and Jury were motioning for me to join them for a posse picture.

"Sure, baby, go ahead and have fun."